EXPLORING THE NUMBERS

1 to 100

Activities, Learning Center Ideas, and Celebrations

by Mary Beth Spann

and the Teachers at the Babylon Elementary School, Babylon, New York

SCHOLASTIC
PROFESSIONAL BOOKS

New York ◆ Toronto ◆ London ◆ Auckland ◆ Sydney

ISBN 0-590-49506-2

Cover design by Vincent Ceci

Cover illustration by Liza Schafer

Interior illustration by Ellen Matlach Hassell and Manuel Rivera

Book design by Ellen Matlach Hassell for Boultinghouse & Boultinghouse, Inc.

Acknowledgments

More than 100 thanks to administration, teachers, parents, and students at the Babylon Elementary School in Babylon, New York, who so generously shared their "100 Day Celebration" project and activity ideas. Special appreciation goes to the following Babylon Elementary professionals who helped make this resource a reality: Donna Cabral, Esther Fusco, Marie Gallay, Donna Grosso, Ingrid Hancock, Donna Harz, Marjorie Hauck, Marsha Kaplowitz, Barbara Krucher, Olivia Merz, Dee Mountcastle, Mary Quinn, Ella Scaife, Dee Schweitzer, and Anita Todd.

Thanks also go to Terry Cooper and Liza Schafer, both Scholastic Professional Book editors, and to mathematics consultant and educational writer Marcia K. Miller for making certain that the suggested activities you find in the book are indeed designed to create hundreds of meaningful and engaging mathematical opportunities for children.

—M. B. S.

Table of Contents

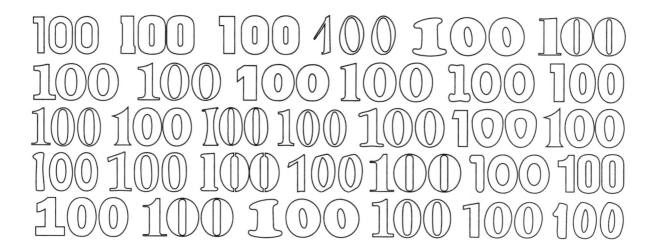

Introduction

Children's natural love of large numbers and penchant for patterning is the inspiration for this book. Here you'll find a year-full of number and pattern-related activities and project possibilities that connect with kids' interests and intellects, while respecting their individual learning needs and levels.

Whether your students and you are beginners or pros at exploring the numbers 1 to 100, you can count on this book to inspire and inform. But before trying any of the activities in this book, it's important that you understand why we should include them in our curriculum and what we want children to learn from them.

From the time they are quite young, children are fascinated with large numbers and large amounts. This wonder is often reflected in children's books and stories. What fun to own 101 dalmatians, to wear Bartholomew Cubbins' 500 hats, or to march 10,000 men to the top of the hill and march them all down again!

A love of big numbers is just one way children demonstrate their growing awareness of the math around them. Children in kindergarten and the early elementary grades are also naturally drawn to shapes and patterns. As they grow, they begin to notice similarities and differences in their concrete and abstract environments. Consequently, youngsters delight in discovering the shape and pattern possibilities that exist in nearly every experience from leaf sorting to storytelling. Such math awareness helps them make sense of their ever-widening world.

Before Beginning

The numbers 1 to 100 are rich with teaching and learning possibilities. By exploring these numbers and how they relate to each other in position and size, children have opportunities to deepen their number sense. This is the greatest goal of each of the activities included here. But this goal isn't achieved by having children complete one or two isolated activities. In fact, mathematicians tell us that children need many and varied opportunities over the duration of a school year (or years) in order to first experience and finally internalize what's been presented to them.

What Children *Don't* Need to Know

Happily, this book is chock-full of the type of activities you'll need to help children experience large numbers in small doses. And to benefit from the activities, students *do not need to be skilled in the reading, writing, or arithmetic of numbers 1 to 100!* For example, to begin exploring the numbers 1 to 100, students do not need:

- to be able to read all the numbers from 1 to 100;
- to be able to write all the numbers from 1 to 100;
- to be able to recognize or identify all the numbers from 1 to 100; or
- to be able to add, subtract, multiply, or divide numbers in order to arrive at correct answers.

It's true that engaging in some of the activities will help students be more aware of numbers and number relationships, but this is a long-range goal, not a prerequisite.

And... What's Nice for You to Know

The activities and teaching tips offered in each section are meant to be enjoyed with your students as you wish. (After all, you know your class best!) Unless otherwise indicated, the activities and projects can be completed by students working alone, in small groups, or by the entire class. Many of the activities described lend themselves beautifully to a cooperative learning setting. There are no right or wrong ways to proceed. But in any event, take your time as you develop each one. The following key points can help guide you through.

- Learning about numbers is a process. Every meaningful interaction or conceptual connection children make about the numbers 1 to 100 does not result in a concrete product.

- The activities in this book provide a wealth of opportunities to have children brainstorm and solve problems. Whenever possible, put your own ideas on hold as you look to your students for fresh insights, inspirations, and direction. Have them decide how to evenly divide the work of creating a "hundreds" display. Even better, allow them to suggest their own interest-based displays and activities. Entertain lots of ideas before deciding together how to proceed.

- Each activity offers a chance to spark dialogue. When working with large numbers and the patterns they form, there is much for children to think and wonder about. Creative questioning techniques on your part can help steer them in the most inquisitive directions. Try popping brain-tickling, open-ended questions, such as:
  - What if...?
  - How can you...?
  - How would you...?
  - How could you...?
  - Do you agree...?
  - Would it be better if...?
  - How many...?
  - What ideas do you have about...?

- Remember, parental support is essential for classroom success. Help parents understand the importance of what you're doing in class by sending home letters outlining your plans. In your letter, stress the importance of process over product. Also, help parents understand that learning the concepts surrounding the numbers 1 to 100 is not the same as being able to recite, write, or recognize the names of the numerals.

Day One and Counting: The Origin of Counting the First 100 Days of School

The popular *Mathematics Their Way* publication by Mary Baratta-Lorton (Addison-Wesley, 1976) and the related Mathematics Their Way workshops and newsletters have long advocated that teachers and students keep track of the first 100 days of their school year. For example, workshop participants are shown how a length of adding-machine tape displayed in the room may be used by students to record each school day, thus creating a number line representing the first 100 days of school.

For each school day, students involved in a Mathematics Their Way approach also place one straw into a "ones" cup affixed to the same bulletin board as the monthly calendar. Each time 10 straws accumulate, they are bundled together with a rubber band and transferred to a "tens" cup located to the left of the ones cup. On the 100th day of school, the 10 bundles of 10 are then ceremoniously transferred to a "hundreds" cup located to the left of the tens cup.

The two Mathematics Their Way experiences described above underscore the importance of letting students see the numbers build day after day, week after week, until they reach 100. How much more effective for students to count 100 straws over a period of 100 days than to limit such counting experiences to only one or two lessons!

Please realize that any time is the right time to launch a classroom focus on large numbers. It isn't always necessary to begin your count on the first day of school—any set of 100 school days will do. Perhaps you'd prefer counting up from January 1? Or counting down the last 50 days of the school year? Lots of creative arrangements are possible. The idea is to help students concentrate on counting numbers over time so that, over time, children can develop the number sense they need to proceed.

Warm Up to 100: Activities to Get Kids Started

Following are teacher-directed, long-range skill- and concept-building activities that lay the foundation for a focus on 100. For the most meaningful learning fun, be sure to include your students in the planning stages of each activity whenever possible. Remember, student input is the best guarantee for student success!

✴ Read 100 Books

Over the course of several weeks or 100 days, read aloud 100 books! To keep track of the number of books you read, have children take turns completing the bookworm reports on page 10. (If they are prewriters, they can dictate their reports to you.) Display a bookworm head with the completed body segments in order around the room or in a hallway. To reinforce concepts of ones, tens, and hundreds, begin a new worm for every 10 body segments.

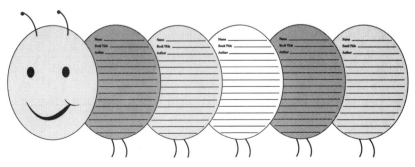

Make the Bookworm Grow!

Name _____

Book Title _____

Author _____

_____

Read a book and then write about your book here. Tell why you did or did not like the book. Then add your report to the bookworm.

_____

_____

_____

_____

_____

_____

_____

_____

✱ Read 100 Poems

Start each morning with a poem until you've read 100! "100 Is a Lot!" by Meish Goldish, on page 12, is a perfect one to get you started. Copy the poem onto chart paper and invite students to read it chorally. If you like, replace some of the couplets with new ones written by your class! (Make sure to maintain the poem's 100 words.) Later, provide students with photocopies of the poem and challenge them to count each of the 100 words.

☑ **TEACHING TIP** Two great sources of poems for the primary grades are *Sing a Song of Popcorn* (Scholastic, 1988) and *Poetry Place Anthology* (Scholastic, 1983).

✱ Tell 100 Stories

Look in books featuring collections of stories to tell. (Flannelboard books are a good resource for tell-aloud stories for young children.) Each time you tell a story, have students take turns using props from the drama corner to act out a favorite scene. Photograph students acting out the scenes and arrange photos in an album labeled "Picture 100 Stories." Label each photograph with the name of the story it represents. Students may then write or dictate a caption to explain each photograph.

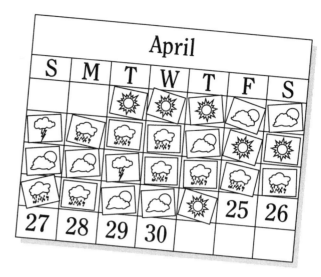

✱ Graph 100 Days of Weather

During a class discussion, decide on the types of weather that are typical in your locale. Then have students choose a simple symbol to represent each weather type (a sun for sunny, a cloud for cloudy, a raindrop for rainy, and so on). Post these symbols on a reference chart next to a monthly calendar. On a nearby table, provide students with a supply of three-inch square sticky notepads and markers. At the end of each day, have students record a weather symbol on a sticky note and then stick it over the appropriate square on the calendar. (The sticky note allows children to peek at the calendar dates when necessary.) When 100 days of weather have accumulated, transfer the sticky notes to a large weather graph.

☑ **TEACHING TIP** If you use a different color notepad for each month, children will be able to easily track the weather for each month on the graph.

☑ **TEACHING TIP** Challenge students to decide what to do when more than one weather type occurs on the same day. Encourage many ideas and have students settle on one way to proceed.

100 Is a Lot!

100 dogs, 100 cats,
100 heads for 100 hats.
100 women, 100 men,
100's more than 5 or 10.
100 buttons, 100 coats,
100 sails for 100 boats.
100 cookies, 100 cakes,
100 kids with bellyaches!
100 shoes, 100 socks,
100 keys for 100 locks.
100 puddles mighty dirty,
100's even more than 30.
100 daughters, 100 sons,
100 franks on 100 buns.
100 trees, 100 plants,
100 picnics, 100 ants!
100 is a lot to count,
100 is a LARGE AMOUNT!
100 kisses, 100 hugs,
100 bats and 100 bugs.
100 bees, 100 birds,
This poem has 100 words!

by Meish Goldish

★ Display Adding-Machine Tape

If you decide to count and record the days of school on adding-machine tape as described on page 8, consider the following different ways of arranging your display:

in one continuous strip around the room;

1	2	3	4	5	6	7	8	9	10	11	12	13	14	15	16

in horizontal rows (ending at every fifth or tenth number), so children can easily spot patterns;

1	2	3	4	5	6	7	8	9	10
11	12	13	14	15	16	17	18	19	20
21	22	23	24	25	26	27	28	29	30

in vertical rows so children can look across to see progressions of tens groupings (1, 11, 21, 31, and so on).

1	11	21
2	12	22
3	13	23
4	14	24
5	15	25
6	16	26
7	17	27
8	18	28
9	19	29
10	20	30

Consider creating more than one adding-machine tape display of days! Have children contribute ideas of their own. Then invite them to compare and contrast arrangements and to notice patterns that each one suggests.

☑ **TEACHING TIP** Use a different color marker to record the days in each month.

★ Calendar Journals

Each month, provide each student with a copy of the blank calendar on page 14, and copies of the journal page on page 15. Each day, after students record the date in the large box, have them use the small boxes provided to record a running record of days from 1 to 100. You may choose to only count the days school is in session, or you may decide to count all the days in each month until you reach 100. Have students use the corresponding journal page to record one happening or event for each calendar day. Bind calendars and journal pages together into booklets labeled "My Journal of 100 Days."

100 Calendar

Name _____

Month: _____

19 18 17 16 15 14 13 12 11 10 9 8 7 6 5 4 3 2 1

21

22 Name_____ **100**

23 99

24 98

25 **Journal** 97

26 **Page** 96

27 95

28 94

Today's date is	Today's number is

29 93

30 92

31 91

32 90

33 89

34 88

35 87

36 86

37 85

38 84

39 83

40 82

41 81

42 80

43 79

44 78

45 77

46 76

47 75

48 74

49 73

50 72

51 71

52 70

53 69

54 55 56 57 58 59 60 61 62 63 64 65 66 67 68

Centering on 100: Activities and Learning Center Ideas

Once you've begun to lay the groundwork for approaching number concepts leading up to and including 100, you'll want to set up a student learning center filled with activities, projects, games, and manipulatives to promote individual and cooperative learning explorations. Here are some ideas to get you started.

★ 100 Chart Patterns

Make copies of the 100 Chart on page 18. Invite students to use copies of the chart to notice patterns they create when they:

- color all the boxes with numbers that contain the numeral 0 (or 1, or 2, or 3, or 4, and so on);
- color every other box;
- color every third box (so that they count and color correctly, suggest that students say the pattern as they work, such as, "One, two, color; three, four color, . . .");
- color all the boxes with numbers containing one digit;
- color all the boxes with numbers containing two digits;
- color all the boxes with numbers containing three digits;
- color all the boxes with numbers containing the numeral 1 (or 2, or 3, . . .) in the one place;
- color all the boxes with numbers containing the numeral 1 (or 2, or 3, . . .) in the tens place; and
- color each diagonal strip of boxes from corner to corner.

✱ 100 Chart Puzzle

Cut apart the 100 Chart (into strips, chunks, or individual boxes) and challenge students to reassemble it. Beginners can use a chart as a puzzle mat/guide, and experienced students can try assembling the puzzle on their own. Different cuts can yield puzzles that reinforce different concepts. For example, make 10 horizontal cuts to explore units of 10. Make irregular cuts (see at right) to reinforce number order.

✱ 100 Chart Bingo

Use copies of the 100 Chart, plus a supply of markers (plastic chips, popcorn kernels, cotton balls), to play these bingo games.

Give each child a copy of the 100 Chart. Ask children to use crayons to lightly shade in any predetermined number of boxes. (Boxes they shade needn't be in a straight line.) Cut one 100 Chart apart and place individual numbers in a shoe box. Draw and call numbers one at a time. Students place markers only on numbers they've colored in. When a student has covered all his or her colored-in numbers, he or she yells "BINGO!" The student must then read back all the numbers called to verify that the win is valid.

☑ **TEACHING TIP** As numbers are called, place number squares over intact chart so you can see at a glance which numbers have been called.

Variation: Cut a chart into quarters or strips. Give each child an identical segment of the chart. Have children use crayons to lightly color in four or five of the number boxes. Then cut apart the individual numbers in one of the same quarters or strips and place into a shoe box. Draw numbers one at a time and call them out. Children use markers to cover only those numbers called that they've colored in. When a student's colored-in numbers are all covered, he or she yells "BINGO!"

✱ More Math Words

Use the 100 Chart to help increase students' math language. Ask students to use the charts as follow-the-directions game boards to locate numbers you describe, such as:

- ◆ find the number that matches the number I'm showing you and trace it on your chart (matching);
- ◆ find the number that comes before, or after, 33 and color it red (order);
- ◆ find the number that comes between 7 and 9 and color it yellow (order);
- ◆ find the number that is one more than, or 2 less than, 12 (addition, subtraction).

☑ **TEACHING TIP** A set of index cards you've numbered 1 to 100 will come in handy when asking students to match numerals.

100 Chart

Name _____

1	2	3	4	5	6	7	8	9	10
11	12	13	14	15	16	17	18	19	20
21	22	23	24	25	26	27	28	29	30
31	32	33	34	35	36	37	38	39	40
41	42	43	44	45	46	47	48	49	50
51	52	53	54	55	56	57	58	59	60
61	62	63	64	65	66	67	68	69	70
71	72	73	74	75	76	77	78	79	80
81	82	83	84	85	86	87	88	89	90
91	92	93	94	95	96	97	98	99	100

18

✱ Fill 100 Boxes

Provide students with copies of the blank 100 Grid (featuring 100 boxes) found on page 20. Invite students to use copies of the chart to:

- print the numbers 1 to 100;

- print 100 fingerprints or pencil-eraser prints (try washable ink pads for prints);

- print combinations of numbers, names, and pictures in groups that reinforce units they're studying. For example, to reinforce fives, a student might fill in five footprints, followed by five numbers, five fingerprints, and so on;

- print the numbers 1 to 100, then color patterns by counting boxes (by twos, by threes, etc.); and/or

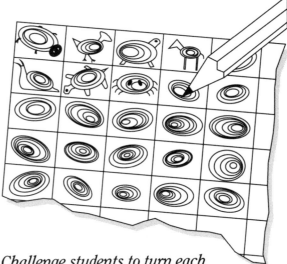

Challenge students to turn each fingerprint into an animal.

1	2	3	4	5	6	7	8	9	10
11	12	13	14	15	16	17	18	19	20
21	22	23	24	25	26	27	28	29	30
31	32	33	34	35	36	37	38	39	40

- create secret pattern puzzles by shading boxes according to number patterns known only to them. Then have students exchange completed number charts and try to guess the number patterns colored in.

☑TEACHING TIP Create a few of these pattern puzzles (as shown in the illustration) with the whole group before asking smaller groups to create their own.

1	2	3	4	5	6
11	12	13	14	15	16
21	22	23	24	25	26
31	32	33	34	35	36
41	42	43	44	45	46
51	52	53	54	55	56

Pattern = Only numbers containing the digit 3 are shaded.

Name _____

✶ The Money Store

Experiences with money offer students some real-life math they can bank on. Set up one corner of your classroom as a bank or a grocery or department store, then use these ideas to get your students shopping.

- Provide students with a table (to use as a checkout counter or a teller's window) and some realistic props (calculator, cash register, adding machine and tape, receipt booklets, bank stationery, and junk-mail envelopes).

- Supply real or pretend money to use.

- Ask children to bring in empty cereal and soap boxes or books and toys to "sell" at the store. (Explain that all items will be returned to their owners.) Then provide students with removable sticky notes and show them how they can use the notes to affix prices they can recognize (5¢, 10¢, 25¢,...) to the merchandise.

Variation: Instead of a store, set up a bank. Let children take turns playing teller, loan officer, and so on. For real-life applications, let the tellers handle lunch money, special trip funds, and so on.

☑**TEACHING TIP** Let children experiment with rolls of coins and loose coins (or play money) to see how many of each coin type is needed to make $1. (For example, 100 pennies equals $1.) Also, show how many combinations of coins can add up to the same total amount of money. Children need lots of experiences with money before they are able to select the correct number of coins needed to add up to a certain amount of money, but seeing you demonstrate the process is a first step to understanding.

✶ The Money Exchange Game

Here's another activity that reinforces the various units represented in a dollar. Offer children copies of the game board on page 22, a pair of dice, and a supply of pennies and dimes (or plastic chips or play money). Have children take turns rolling the dice and counting out the number of pennies indicated on the dice. The player then places the coins or chips on the corresponding game board spot. When the row of pennies is filled, the player exchanges the pennies for a dime. When the row of dimes is filled, the player exchanges it for a dollar. The first student to make exchanges up to one dollar wins.

Money Exchange Game

Pennies

1    6

2   7

3   8

4   9

5   10

Dimes

1   6

2   7

3   8

4   9

5   10

Dollar

✱ Structures

Offer groups of students a limited number (10, 20, 25, 50, 100) of building supplies such as connecting cubes, small plastic stacking bricks, cardboard bricks, paper or plastic cups, empty plastic yogurt cups, empty plastic deli containers, and so on, and challenge them to incorporate all the pieces into one structure. Or offer each group a different number of the same-type supply (group 1 receives 25 unit blocks, group 2 receives 50 unit blocks, and group 3 receives 100 unit blocks). After structures are complete, have students describe, compare, and contrast results. Use the opportunity to build math talk into their vocabularies: "I see more blocks in this structure and less blocks in this structure," or, "This structure is tall, this one is taller, and this one is the tallest!"

More Structure Ideas

- Correspond the number of building supplies the children work with to the number of days counted in your count-up to 100.

- Repeat the activity posing a variety of problems. For example, have students use a set number of supplies and challenge them to build the tallest, the strongest, or the longest structure possible. When structures are complete, label each one with a descriptive sign telling how the student made the structure tall, strong, or long. If structures are not permanent, consider photographing each one and displaying photos and descriptions in a class gallery.

✱ 100 Toilet-Paper Rolls

Challenge students to collect a specific number (from 1 to 100) of empty toilet-paper rolls to use in making a three-dimensional stand-up design such as a tree or the numeral representing the number of tubes used. Rolls may be glued to each other, and then to oaktag or cardboard. (Before gluing rolls together, students can experiment with roll arrangements.) Try stuffing tissue paper into tubes for designs that require hair or leaves. If desired, cut rolls in half before gluing.

☑**TEACHING TIP** Ask students to predict how many half-size rolls will result from cutting their entire collection in half.

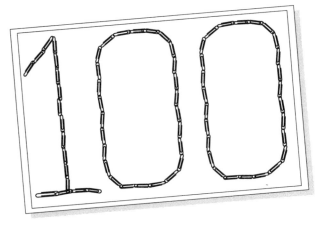

✱ 100 Connecting Links or Paper Clips

Offer students a supply of paper clips or plastic connecting links (available from school-supply companies specializing in math manipulatives). Staple a length of self-adhesive paper (sticky side out) to a bulletin board. Invite students to press the clips or links onto the self-adhesive paper to create a picture or to spell a message.

Or have students use links or color-coated paper clips to create colorful pattern mobiles. Each mobile should contain 100 clips. Children might choose to display 4 sets of 25 clips or 10 sets of 10 clips.

☑ **TEACHING TIP** Add tape to the end of the hanger to prevent accidents.

Students may also connect links or clips to measure how tall they are. How many clips more or less than 100 did each student need to measure his or her height?

✱ 100 Stars

Ask students to use foil stars and black construction or craft paper to create illustrations and designs (for example, of constellations), or to spell out starry messages. Before gluing stars on the paper, have students sketch their ideas and then make placement dots on the black background with white or yellow chalk. Display star-studded papers together with labels indicating how many stars are in each picture, and a running tabulation showing how many stars are displayed in all.

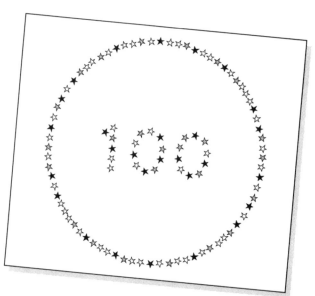

✱ Dragon Dice

Reproduce and assemble the set of Dragon Dice on page 25. To play the game, divide students into two teams. Have students on one team take turns rolling the dice as many times as they wish. The number appearing on the dice becomes the team's score and is recorded as a running tabulation on a nearby chalkboard by you. If one dragon face appears, the most recent addition to that team's score is subtracted and play is passed to the other team. If both dragon faces appear, the team loses its entire score and play is passed to the other team. The first team to reach 100 (or any other predetermined score) wins.

To assemble the Dragon Dice:
1. Cut out the dice along the solid lines.
2. Fold the dice along the dashed lines.
3. Paste or tape the tabs to form the dice.

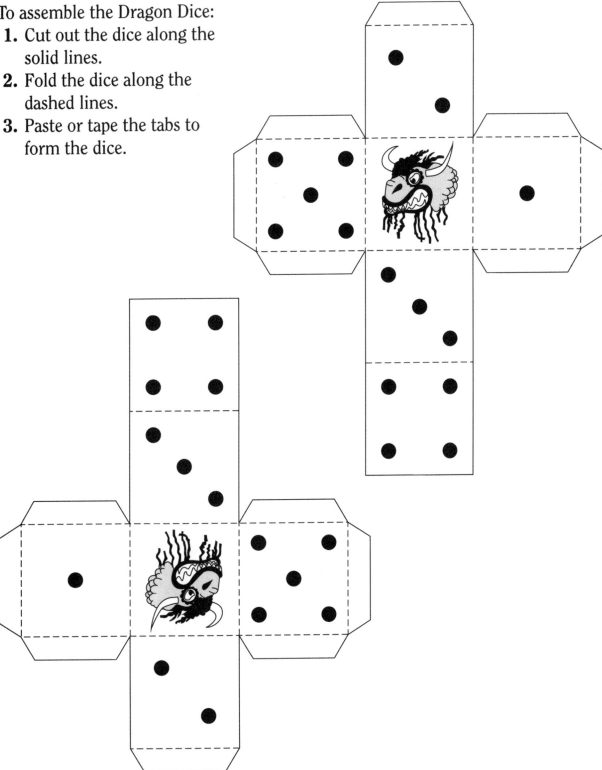

✱ 100 Stickers

Save stickers and seals (available through give-away offers and in junk-mail advertisements). Have groups of students incorporate stickers and seals into a collage representing a theme such as animals, flowers, colors, faces, and so on. If you do not have 100 stickers for each group, supply students with what you have and challenge them to draw in the remaining number of stickers needed to make 100. Or create collages based on other units of 100, using 25 or 50 stickers, for example. Ask children for their input on the best ways to keep track of the numbers involved in creating their 100 collages.

✱ 100 Stampers

Offer students rubber stampers featuring pictures, letters, or numbers; ink pads (the washable variety); and paper (prepared with a blank grid, if desired). Ask children to stamp 100 images.

Variation 1: To explore other units up to and including 100, ask one group of children to stamp 100 images in groups of 10, another in groups of 25, and so on. Have students use a different color stamp for each set to help make the number of sets stand out.

Variation 2: Offer children four or five different colored stamp pads and only one stamp shape. Challenge children to use the stamp and the colors to create a color pattern of 100 stamps. Then ask them how many of each color they used. Help students create number sentences by adding the number of colored images together to equal 100.

✱ 100 Prints

Offer children sponge shapes and paint for printing 100 shapes. Ask students to experiment with designs and patterns. Any variation of the following medium and material offerings will produce interesting and varied results: one sponge shape and many colors of paint, many sponge shapes and one color paint, multiple sponge shapes and multiple colors of paint.

★ 100 Facts

When researching a theme or topic, students can record bits of information on sticky notes and then post these notes on chart paper. Aim to collect a predetermined number (such as 100, 50, 25, . . .) of facts. Flag each fact with a shape symbol cut from construction paper. Label the shapes with numbers 1 to 100.

> 1 Dinosaurs ate plants and meat.
>
> 2 Dinosaurs became extinct 65 million years ago.

★ 100 Scavenger Hunt

Select one or more criteria and have students hunt, in or out of the classroom, for a specific number of related objects (which may or may not add up to 100). Try generating a list of student-suggested criteria before deciding on objects to hunt for.

Here are some suggested criteria to try:
- colors;
- geometric shapes;
- pointy (or smooth, rough, high, low, hard, soft, and so on) things; and
- objects with numerals printed on them.

★ Cards Count

Hide playing cards around your classroom. Challenge children to hunt until they locate the cards. The numbers featured on each card count as points, with aces equaling 1 point, picture cards equaling 0 points, and other cards equaling their face values. Help students add up their individual scores. Highest (or lowest) score wins. Challenge children to create groups with combined scores that add up to 100 (or 25, or 50, . . .).

★ 100 T-shirt Decorations

At the beginning of the school year (or at the beginning of your 100-day count), have each student bring in a plain, inexpensive T-shirt. Provide students with fabric paint and sponge shapes (optional) and have them each print 100 handprints (or stars, or happy faces, or hearts, etc.) on their shirts. Students may add one shape per day, or may complete their shirts in one or two printing sessions.

☑**TEACHING TIP** So that students can easily keep track of how many prints they make, and to reinforce the concept of sets and multiples, provide different color paint for each set of 10 prints.

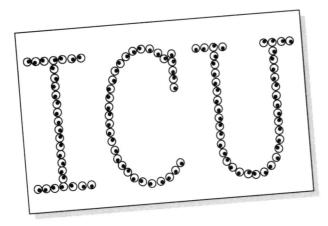

★ 100 Googly Eyes

Divide 100 googly eyes among the students (watch for post-holiday sales on eyes). Have students work together to glue the eyes down to spell a message or incorporate the eyes into a mural. Some ideas for a mural include a farm scene, an underwater sea-life scene, and favorite characters from literature. Or try dividing the 100 eyes among all of the students, having them use the eyes to create mini-posters on which a groundline has been predrawn and then displaying the posters together to form one continuous illustration.

★ 100 People We Know and Love

Have students work together to create a mural of "100 People We Know and Love," including 100 drawings and/or photos of people the children know personally, such as family members, friends, school personnel, and community helpers.

★ 100 Faces

Have the class work together to figure out how many faces each child needs to decorate to equal a total of 100 faces. Then provide students with oval-shaped templates (cut from oaktag or scrap cardboard), construction paper, and markers. Have students trace and cut ovals from the construction paper, and then use markers to add features to the faces. Display faces together on a bulletin board or doorway.

☑**TEACHING TIP** When decorating the faces, students will enjoy referring to drawing books such as *Ed Emberly's Drawing Book of Faces* (Little, Brown, 1974) for inspiration.

Variation 1: In addition to ovals, provide students with a variety of geometric shapes to trace and decorate as faces. Have students decide how to represent the same number of faces cut from each of the geometric shapes to equal 100 in all. So if students are working with 5 different shapes, they can decorate 20 of each shape to make 100 faces.

Variation 2: Have students decide how to represent the same number of faces cut from each color (instead of each shape) of construction paper to equal 100 in all.

☑**TEACHING TIP** Ask students for their input on deciding how to best divide up the work of cutting and decorating faces.

★ 100 Things in a Basket (photo essay)

Provide each group of students with a small basket (or box or wide-mouthed plastic container) and a collection of objects (marbles, pencils, crayons, straws, pipe cleaners, markers, blocks, toys, counters, wrapped candies, and so on). Challenge each group to try fitting 100 of its assigned object into the basket. First, have them estimate how many of the 100 will fit (or how many groups of 10, 20, and so on). Encourage students to discuss and experiment with the different shapes and sizes. If they want to fit 100, what's the best way to proceed? Photograph the basket filled (or overflowing) with each object collection. Which objects fit and which don't? Place photos into a small album and have the children dictate or write descriptive captions for each photo.

☑**TEACHING TIP** If students' first attempts at fitting 100 of any one object or combination of objects into the container are unsuccessful, challenge them to decide if another arrangement might do the trick.

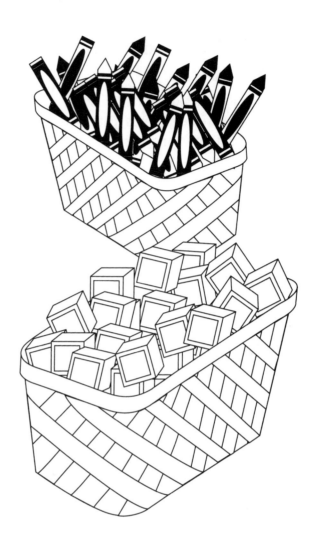

100 Things in a Basket by Mrs. Marshall's class

★ Centenarian Guest

If possible, consider having a centenarian visit your class. Have children prepare a list of questions to ask your guest. Students might be interested to know how daily life 100 years ago differs from daily life at the present time. After the visit, students might want to brainstorm a list of ways life might be different when they are 100 years old.

☑**TEACHING TIP** If a visit with a centenarian isn't possible, consider corresponding with a 100-year-old friend. Check with your local historical society for names.

✱ 100 Craft Sticks or Toothpicks

Have students glue down craft sticks (or toothpicks) to create pictures, patterns, or messages. Toothpicks may also be stuck into lumps of clay or upside-down egg-carton cups to create sculptures.

Variation 1: Challenge children to create a series of pictures of one object, such as a house, first using 10 sticks, then 20, then 30 (or 5, then 10, etc.). How do the details in the pictures change as the number of sticks increases?

Variation 2: Reinforce visual estimation skills by having students count out a number of toothpicks, say 10, then try to pick up a different group of 10 without counting. Encourage children to share their techniques (for example, one student might use a toothpick to measure how much space 10 toothpicks takes up, another might go by feel, and so on). Extend by having students try to estimate 20 toothpicks.

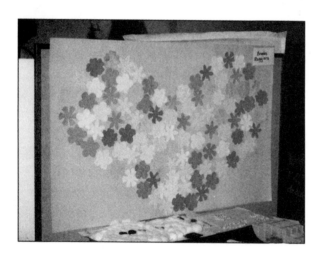

✱ 100 Geometric Shapes

Have students work in cooperative groups to incorporate 100 precut construction-paper shapes (circles, squares, triangles, rectangles) into pictures or designs. After gluing shapes to poster-size pieces of oaktag or craft paper, students can use the graph on page 31 to show how many of each shape they used to complete their pictures.

Variation: Instead of the geometric shapes suggested above, try precutting other shapes such as ovals, parallelograms, pentagons, hexagons, animals, flowers, and so on.

100 Geometric Shapes Graph

Name _____

	1	2	3	4	5	6	7	8	9	10	11	12	13	14	15	16	17	18	19	20	21	22	23	24	25	26	27	28	29	30	31	32	33	34	35
◯																																			
▢																																			
◁																																			
▭																																			

★ 99+1 Collage Puzzles

Provide students with discarded magazines. (Nature magazines and magazines featuring recipes work well for this activity.) Have students work to collect and cut out 99 pictures related to one subject, topic, or theme (dogs, favorite snack foods, people's faces, faraway places, etc.). Then have students locate one picture that is in direct opposition to the 99 others; for example, collect 99 dog pictures and one cat picture. Provide a large piece of oaktag and have students glue pictures down collage-style (with the large pictures glued down first, followed by smaller pictures). Pictures should overlap slightly. Have students write or dictate a corresponding caption for each collage such as: "99 Dogs Plus 1 Cat—Can You Find the Cat?"

Other ideas for picture collages include:

- 99 birds + 1 cat
- 99 wild animals + 1 stuffed animal
- 99 children + 1 adult
- 99 mammals + 1 reptile
- 99 alphabet letters + 1 number

★ Coins and Chips

Offer students a set of 100 coins (pennies) or 100 plastic counting chips. Have students glue coins or chips down on cardboard or oaktag to spell messages or to make pictures. To preserve coin arrays before disassembling (coins may be washed and put back into circulation), have students place a piece of thin copy or drawing paper over the array and rub the paper with the side of a crayon to produce a rubbing of the 100 coins.

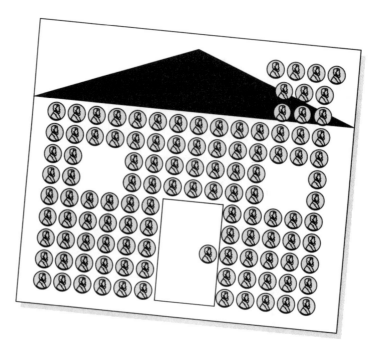

★ 100 Buttons

Have students take turns sewing buttons onto T-shirts or creating a classroom button banner by sewing buttons onto a length of burlap. Before sewing, have students decide on their own criteria (large, small, fancy, plain, etc.) for sorting the buttons to determine how many of each type of button add up to 100.

☑**TEACHING TIP** 100 identical buttons sewn on a T-shirt or banner make for an impressive display. Look for sales on buttons in craft and sewing supply stores. Large, flat buttons with two or four holes pierced through are easiest for students to work with.

★ Necklaces

Supply students with materials to make 100-piece necklaces. Students will need plastic craft needles, elastic thread, and circular-shaped cereals or candies. Plastic beads and segments cut from plastic straws also work well. To help students understand how 10 groups of 10 equal 100, provide students with one-inch square paper space markers they may thread on their necklaces following each group of 10 (and then tear off when the necklace is complete).

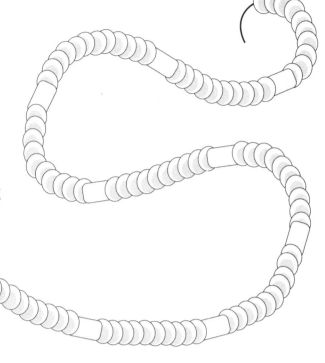

★ 100 Piece Lovey Bug

Cut 101 heart shapes from construction paper. Decorate one heart to represent the head. Ask the children to divide the remaining 100 hearts so that each student has the same number of hearts to decorate as he or she wishes. Display head and body parts together in a long, continuous line.

☑**TEACHING TIP** Have students use hearts to make picture collages of things they love. Or ask students to bring in photos of loved ones. Make photocopies of the photos and have students glue photos to their hearts.

✱ 100 Bottle Caps

Have students collect 100 caps from juice and soft-drink bottles. Then brainstorm ways the caps can be incorporated into a poster display. For example, when glued onto oaktag or poster board, caps could represent wheels on vehicles, balloons, spots on a clown's outfit, flower centers (for a garden motif), or people's heads.

☑**TEACHING TIP** Before gluing caps in place, have students experiment with cap placement possibilities on the oaktag or poster board. When satisfied with the arrangement, have students use a pencil to trace each cap's placement. Have students use markers to add details to the display.

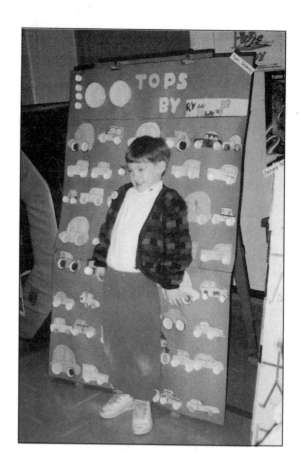

✱ 100 Baby-Food Jar Caps

Collect 100 baby-food jar caps. Give students paper cutouts that fit inside the caps. Have students create mini works of art and glue them inside the caps. Attach self-sticking magnetic strips to the back of each jar lid and display the lids on a magnetic bulletin board or cookie sheets. Students may then take their own lid creations home to use as refrigerator magnets.

☑**TEACHING TIP** For a permanent classroom display, attach completed caps to a piece of thin plywood using a hot-glue gun. Artists may then substitute new artwork for old by gluing newly decorated circles over old ones.

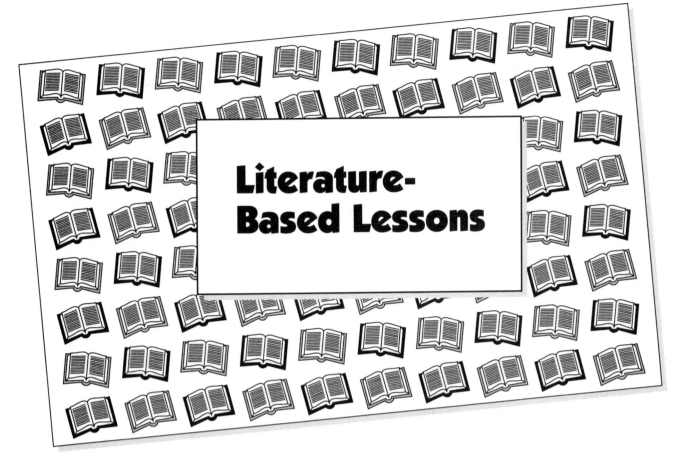

Literature-
Based Lessons

Many favorite books double as springboards to exploring
numbers 1 to 100. This section features book selections
and literature-based follow-ups to get you started.

The Grouchy Ladybug

by Eric Carle (HarperCollins, 1986)

"Hey you," said the grouchy ladybug. "Want to fight?"
This ladybug challenges any animal that crosses her
path, no matter how big. The timing of each encounter
corresponds to small clocks incorporated into the
illustrations, making the story a natural for math
connections.

✱ 100-Dot Ladybug

Construct a 100-dot ladybug. First cut two large oval shapes from red
craft paper. Staple shapes together, matching edges and leaving a 12-inch
opening. Stuff crumpled newspaper through opening and then staple
shut. Using a brush stroke of black tempera paint, divide the ladybug in
half lengthwise to create wings. Glue a semicircle of black craft paper to

the smaller end of the oval to create a head. Add paper antennae. Paint cardboard tubes (saved from wrapping paper) black, cut them into small segments, and glue to the underside of the bug to create legs. Cut 100 circles of cardboard or oaktag approximately 5 inches in diameter. Ask students to decide how to divide circles evenly among themselves. Then ask students to decorate their circles with black color or black textured art materials (felt, sequins, fabric, paint, etc.). Glue the 100 decorated circles to the ladybug's body.

EXTENSION ACTIVITY
Spot the Spots

Ladybugs aren't the only animals with spots. Challenge students to identify and describe as many spotted animals as they can. Frogs, cheetahs, pythons, giraffes, and their own pets are just a few of the possibilities. Then create a Spot Zoo containing 100 animals with spots.

Millions of Cats

by Wanda Gag (Scholastic, 1928)

This Newbery Honor book tells the classic story of a very old man and a very old woman who are very lonely. "If only we had a cat!" sighs the woman. So the man sets out to get a cat. But instead of one, he brings home hundreds, thousands, millions, and trillions of irresistible cats—or are they?

★ 100 Cats in a Basket

Enlarge the basket shape on page 37. Trace the shape onto craft paper and cut out the basket (it should be approximately 8 feet wide and 4 feet high). Enlarge the cat shape. Trace and cut out 100 cat shapes from construction or manila paper.

Variation 1: Divide cat shapes into sets of 10, 20, or 25. Have children decorate each set to resemble a different type of cat (striped cats, black cats, calico cats, etc.) or to feature a different medium (markers, paint, collage, etc.).

Variation 2: Trace and cut sets representing different sizes (50 large cats and 50 small cats, and so on).

Variation 3: Have students glue their school photos onto the cats' faces.

EXTENSION ACTIVITY
Cat Tales

Create a Cat Tales learning center. Offer a changing selection of books about cats, a cat shape for students to trace, and a literature log (sheets of paper stapled together). Have students log in each time they visit the center (recording the date, the books they are reading, the pages they start and finish on, something they learned, and something they still want to know). Invite students to write cat facts they want to share on cat shapes they trace and cut out; then display at the learning center. Aim for 100 facts to share.

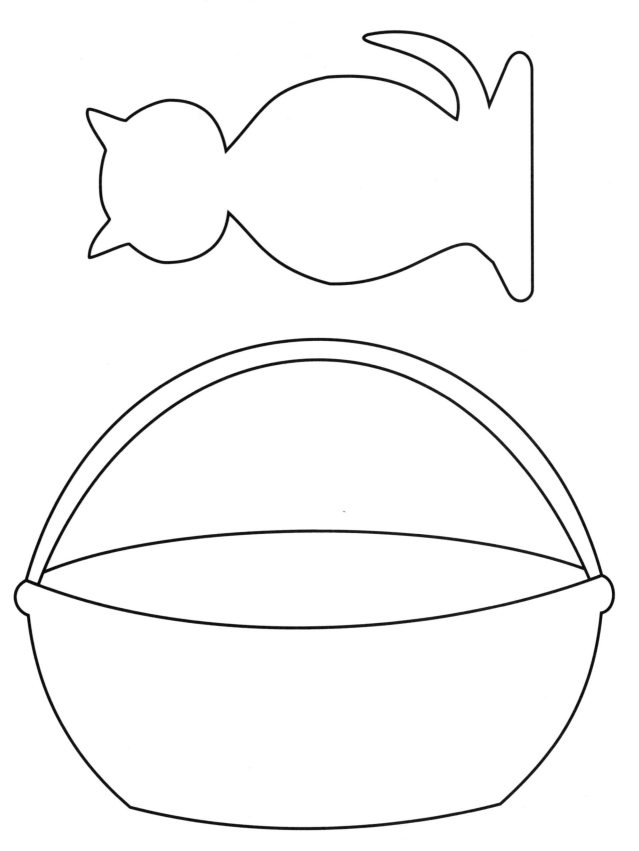

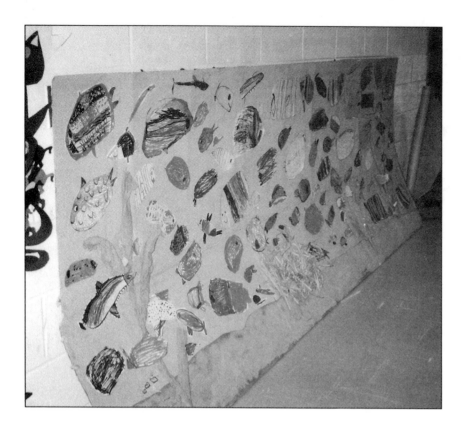

Ocean Parade: A Counting Book

by Patricia MacCarthy (Dial, 1990)

"1 big fish, 2 little fish, 3 flat fish, 4 thin fish, 5 fat fish...." Counting continues by ones up to 19, then by twenties to 100. Dive into this aquatic adventure to explore color, size, and shape, as well.

★ 100 Underwater Creatures

Together, calculate the number of sea animals represented in the book. Then, using a length of blue craft paper to represent an ocean backdrop, have students fill the ocean with 100 underwater creatures they draw, cut, and color themselves. Clumps of shredded green paper attached to the bottom edge of the paper ocean lends a realistic feel to the display.

EXTENSION ACTIVITIES

How Many Ways Can You Count?

Review the way this book counts to 100 (by ones and by twenties). Challenge children to think of more ways to count to 100 (by twos, by fives, by tens, and so on). Encourage children to explain their thinking.

The Facts About Fish

Can fish live on land? Lungfish can! Challenge children to find 99 more amazing facts about fish. You might do a fish-fact-a-day, inviting a different student each day to share information. Write each fact on a fish-shaped cutout and post around the room, in the lunchroom, or in the library.

Caps for Sale

by Ephyr Slobodkina (HarperCollins, 1940)

"Caps! Caps for sale! Fifty cents a cap!" This peddler carries his wares on top of his head—first his own checkered cap, then grey caps, brown caps, then blue, and red. One day, when business is slow, he takes a nap under a tree. When he wakes up, the caps are all gone! Who's responsible for the monkey business? Monkeys, of course!

✱ 100 Caps for Sale

Read *Caps for Sale*. Then, using the patterns on page 40, cut 100 monkey shapes and 100 cap shapes from drawing paper. Invite students to add details to both. Cut a large tree shape and attach it to a bulletin board. Display monkeys wearing caps in and around the tree.

EXTENSION ACTIVITY
Celebrate Hats

Hold a 100 Hats Day. Ask each child to bring in several hats on a specified day. (Make sure you have a total of 100.) Use their hats as a springboard to cross-curricular activities. For example:

- Allow time for children to examine characteristics of the hats and to experiment with different ways to group them. What kinds of patterns can children create using their hats?

- Use the hats to make a live graph of characteristics such as hats with tassels, hats with brims, knit hats, baseball caps, and so on.

- Have students write detailed descriptions of their hats on slips of paper. Put all papers in a hat, display hats together, and let children take turns pulling a slip, reading the description, and trying to identify the hat.

Monkey and Cap Shapes

If You Give a Mouse a Cookie

by Laura Joffe Numeroff (HarperCollins, 1985)

The consequences of giving a mouse a chocolate-chip cookie are described in fast-paced, logical form.

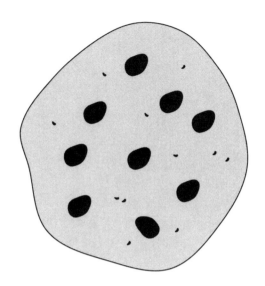

✱ Class-Size Cookie

Use your favorite cookie recipe to bake up a class-size cookie filled or decorated with 100 chocolate chips. Just spread the dough on a greased pizza pan and bake as directed. While students enjoy their treat, share the story.

EXTENSION ACTIVITY

Sweets Survey

What's your favorite cookie? This simple question can pave the way for counting activities and more. Plan, for example, to have students ask 100 schoolmates, teachers, and support staff to name their favorite cookie (or their favorite sweet). Before students gather their data, ask them to predict how chocolate-chip cookies will fare. Present findings on a picture graph and write up the results for a class or school newsletter.

FAVORITE COOKIE	
chocolate-chip	🍪🍪🍪🍪🍪🍪🍪
graham cracker	⬜⬜
gingersnap	⬭⬭⬭
cream-filled	⬛⬛⬛⬛⬛
sugar wafer	▱▱▱▱

✱ 100 Bricks in Humpty Dumpty's Wall

Share the nursery rhyme about Humpty Dumpty, then together recreate the scene of the fall. Begin by asking children to save 100 milk cartons. (Cartons with red print look most brick-like.) When you've collected 100 cartons, help children observe how bricks are stacked in a real wall. Attach cartons together using a hot-glue gun, or punch four holes in each carton and attach from the inside by slipping brass fasteners through the holes. Make your wall 10 cartons wide by 10 cartons high. Enlarge the Humpty Dumpty pattern on page 43. Then cut Humpty's front and back (approximately 3 feet high by 2 feet wide) from white craft paper. After students have decorated Humpty using paints and markers, staple front and back of Humpty together (leaving bottom open as shown in illustration), stuff with crumpled newspapers, and glue to front and back of wall. Add paper legs and shoes.

EXTENSION ACTIVITY

100 Rhymes

Share several nursery rhymes with students. (If you like, read a different rhyme each day for 100 days!) Then challenge students to brainstorm 100 sets of rhyming words such as *bear, stare; house, mouse; plum, glum;* and so on. Write the rhyming word sets on a piece of oaktag and post in an accessible place. Encourage students to use this rhyming word bank for their writing. The bank can also be used to help you and your students write class-created nursery rhymes.

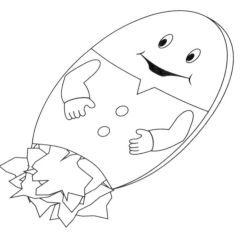

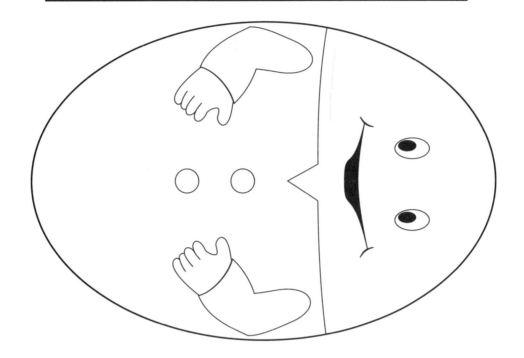

List of Books for Exploring 100

Anno's Counting House by Mitsumasa Anno (Putnam, 1982)

The Boy Who Was Followed Home by Margaret Mahy (Dial, 1986)

A Cache of Jewels and Other Collective Nouns by Ruth Heller (Putnam, 1989)

From One to One Hundred by Teri Sloat (Dutton, 1991)

How Many Feet in the Bed? by Diane Johnston Hamm (Simon & Schuster, 1991)

How Many Stars in the Sky? by Lenny Hort (William Morrow, 1991)

The Icky Bug Counting Book by Jerry Pallotta (Charlesbridge, 1992)

Moja Means One: A Swahili Counting Book (Dial, 1971)

The Philharmonic Gets Dressed by Karla Kuskin (HarperCollins, 1982)

One Gorilla by Atsuko Morozumi (Farrar, Straus & Giroux, 1990)

Over in the Meadow by Olive Wadsworth (Penguin, 1986)

17 Kings and 42 Elephants by Margaret Mahy (Dial, 1990)

Ten Black Dots by Donald Crews (Greenwillow, 1986)

10 for Dinner by Jo Ellen Bogart (Scholastic, 1989)

Ten Nine Eight by Molly Bang (Greenwillow, 1983)

10 Things I Know About Penguins by Wendy Wax and Thomas Payne (Contemporary Books, 1986)

The 329th Friend by Marjorie Weinman Sharmat (Four Winds, 1979)

Twelve Ways to Get to Eleven by Eve Merriam (Simon & Schuster, 1993)

100 Across the Curriculum

Activities involving numbers 1 to 100 can easily crisscross your curriculum. Here are some ideas to get you integrating.

★ Writing

1. Generate lists of 100 items, such as:
   - 100 words that I can write
   - 100 words that begin with *S*
   - 100 ways to show you care
   - 100 favorite foods
   - 100 reasons to love school
   - 100 things I hate to do
   - Things I want 100 of
   - Things I don't want 100 of

2. **Make Topsy-Turvy Books** Use a spiral-bound chart pad to create a book of opposites. Reading from front to back, the book might tell about 50 things to do when it rains; and from back to front, the book might tell about 50 things to do when the sun shines. Have children write or dictate their ideas onto each page, then number and illustrate their entries. Here are some additional topsy-turvy ideas to try:
   - 50 Hot Things/50 Cold Things
   - 50 High Things/50 Low Things
   - 50 Things I Want to Do When I Grow Up/50 Things I Don't Want to Do When I Grow Up
   - 50 Huge Things/50 Tiny Things
   - 50 Hard Things/50 Soft Things
   - 50 Red Things/50 Blue Things

✱ Science

1. **Growing Pains** Observe the first 100 days of the growth of seeds, sprouts, or cuttings. Have students keep 100-day logs, or measure and graph the plant's height at key points, such as every 10 days.

2. **Seed Collections** Have students count out 100 seeds representing a variety of plants.

   ☑**TEACHING TIP** Egg-carton cups make great storage and display receptacles.

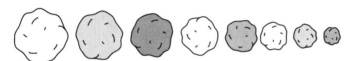

3. Have students collect 100 pebbles and then arrange them in descending size order. Repeat the exercise using shells, pinecones, or leaves.

4. **100 Animals** Have students list 100 different animals. Draw or cut out pictures of each animal. Glue them to a piece of poster board.

5. **Recycle 100** Collect and return 100 beverage containers. Donate refunded deposit money to a favorite charity.

6. **Pick up the Pieces** Pick up 100 pieces of litter on the playground.

   ☑**TEACHING TIP** When conducting garbage pickup, supervise students closely and have students wear gloves.

✱ Music and Movement

1. Have students make a running list titled "100 Things a Body Can Do." Do them!

2. Tell 100 act-outable stories for students to try.

3. Listen to 100 pieces of music.

4. Have students discover physical feats they can perform 100 times, such as hop on one foot, jump rope, dribble a ball, jog in place, and so on.

✱ Social Studies and Geography

1. Share 100 books, stories, and poems from other cultures.

2. Generate a cookbook of 100 recipes from other cultures and countries. Ask children to contribute family recipes.

3. Tell 100 stories about real people. Have students each contribute stories about the characters in their families.

4. Devote a large bulletin board to creating a local map of your school's neighborhood. Every day for 100 days, add one detail to the map—a locale, a street sign, a building. Have students take turns making suggestions for details (including self-portraits) to add to the map.

5. Name 100 places your students have visited.

Culminating Celebration

Mark your count-up efforts with a school-wide 100 Day Celebration, including a Hundreds Hall of Fame display showcasing individual and group projects. Here are some tips for planning and proceeding.

1. Send home ideas for individual student projects (to be completed at home, brought back to school, and displayed at the Hundreds Hall of Fame). Idea suggestions include:

   - collections of 100 items;
   - 100 pennies glued down to make a turtle, a dinosaur, etc.;
   - a taped interview with 100 questions asked of family members;
   - 100 items glued in a straight line to create a measurement tool (use ribbon, adding-machine tape, etc.);
   - 100 seeds glued down to make a picture or a message;
   - 100 family or vacation photos;
   - 100 snacks (raisins, candies, pretzels, cookies, etc.).

   ☑**TEACHING TIP** In your message home, make it clear that these are only suggestions, and that innovative projects are encouraged.

2. On day 91, begin a 10-day countdown to day 100. Make copies of the badges on page 48. Then have students cut out, decorate, and wear the badges.

3. Devote a large space (auditorium, hallway, empty classroom, etc.) to creating a Hundreds Hall of Fame display. A day or two before the celebration, set up the individual and class displays on tables for visitors to view. Displays should all be clearly marked with contributors' names.

4. Design invitations to your Hundreds Hall of Fame. Send to other students, teachers, administrators, and parents.

☑ **TEACHING TIP** If a large number of visitors will be touring your Hall of Fame, consider inviting them at staggered intervals so that displays are easily seen by all.

5. As they arrive for the festivities, try welcoming guests with a 100 Hands Walk-Through display. Cover a large rectangular piece of cardboard (cut from the side of a refrigerator carton, for example) with craft paper and paint on the numeral 100 (large enough to allow children to step through the cutout zeros). Use a craft knife to cut out the middle of the zeros. Have students trace and cut 100 hand shapes from fadeless paper. Glue these to the numerals. On the day of your celebration tie the walk-through to two anchors such as heavy chairs or portable basketball hoops. Stabilize the display by placing a desk or two in back. Assign a parent volunteer to greet students with a hearty "Happy One Hundred Day!" salutation as he or she helps each child step through to the festivities.

6. Offer visitors 100 Day refreshments such as pretzel sticks and bagels (representing the numeral 100), plus cups containing 100 milliliters of juice. You may also bake a large cake decorated with 100 candles.

7. In addition to the snack ideas above, students may wear necklaces comprised of 100 stringable snacks (circular cereal, mini-pretzels, dried fruit, etc.). It's best to have students string these ahead of time so they can nibble as they tour the Hundreds Hall of Fame with their families.

ONLY **10** MORE DAYS!

ONLY **9** MORE DAYS!

ONLY **8** MORE DAYS!

ONLY **7** MORE DAYS!

ONLY **6** MORE DAYS!

ONLY **5** MORE DAYS!

ONLY **4** MORE DAYS!

ONLY **3** MORE DAYS!

ONLY **2** MORE DAYS!

ONLY **1** MORE DAY!

TODAY IS THE **100**TH DAY OF SCHOOL!